P9-DGU-830

EEK & ACK OOZE SLINGERS FROM OUTER SPACE

Librarian Reviewer
Allyson A. W. Lyga, MS
Library Media/Graphic Novel Consultant
Fulbright Memorial Fund Scholar, author

Reading Consultant
Elizabeth Stedem
Educator/Consultant, Colorado Springs, CO
MA in Elementary Education, University of Denver, CO

STONE ARCH BOOKS
MINNEAPOLIS   SAN DIEGO

Graphic Sparks are published by Stone Arch Books,
151 Good Counsel Drive, P.O. Box 669,
Mankato, Minnesota 56002.
www.stonearchbooks.com

Library of Congress Cataloging-in-Publication Data
Hoena, B. A.
    Ooze Slingers from Outer Space / by Blake A. Hoena; illustrated by Steve Harpster.
    p. cm. — (Graphic Sparks. Eek and Ack)
    ISBN-13: 978-1-59889-315-1 (library binding)
    ISBN-10: 1-59889-315-7 (library binding)
    ISBN-13: 978-1-59889-410-3 (paperback)
    ISBN-10: 1-59889-410-2 (paperback)
    1. Graphic novels. I. Harpster, Steve. II. Title.
PN6727.H57O69 2007
741.5'973—dc22   2006028027

Summary: Eek and Ack, the Terrible Twins from the Great Goo Galaxy, are at it again!
They make more plans to conquer Earth, but this time something sticky gets in the way.
And it has eyes! And feet! And it's got the bug-eyed brothers trapped on an asteroid!

Art Director: Heather Kindseth
Graphic Designer: Brann Garvey

For my nephews Ryan, Chase, and Carter,
here's another book to read on our camping
trips — just don't eat the snottle bugs!

1 2 3 4 5 6 11 10 09 08 07 06

Printed in the United States of America

EEK & ACK OOZE SLINGERS FROM OUTER SPACE

by Blake A. Hoena

illustrated by Steve Harpster

Cast of Characters

Eek

Ack

Oozie

23

ABOUT THE AUTHOR

Blake A. Hoena once spent a whole weekend just watching his favorite science-fiction movies. Those movies made him wonder what kind of aliens, with their death rays and hyper-drives, couldn't actually conquer Earth. That's when he created Eek and Ack, who play at conquering Earth like earthling kids play at stopping bad guys. Blake has written more than twenty books for children, and currently lives in Roseville, Minnesota.

ABOUT THE ILLUSTRATOR

Steve Harpster has loved to draw funny cartoons, mean monsters, and goofy gadgets since he was able to pick up a pencil. In first grade, he was able to avoid his writing assignments by working on the pictures for stories instead. Steve was able to land a job drawing funny pictures for books, and that's really what he's best at. Steve lives in Columbus, Ohio, with his wonderful wife, Karen, and their sheepdog, Doodle.

GLOSSARY

asteroid (AS-tuh-royd)—a large rock floating in outer space; some asteroids are found between Mars and Jupiter in an area known as the asteroid belt.

observatory (uhb-ZUR-vuh-tor-ee)—a building used to study stars and the sky with telescopes and other scientific instruments

sinister plot (SIN-iss-tur PLAHT)—an evil plan, such as a plan to destroy Earth

telescope (TEL-uh-skope)—an instrument that makes things that are very far away seem closer and larger; telescopes are used to study stars and planets.

vaporize (VAY-pur-eyez)—to destroy something by turning it into smaller pieces or into dust

EEK AND ACK'S GALAXY OF FACTS

Scientists call that sticky stuff in your nose "mucus." It's also known as snot, boogers, goobers, phlegm, and loogies.

There are four pairs of open spaces in your skull near your nose. The spaces are called "sinuses." Sinuses are snot factories where mucus is produced.

Your sinuses produce about one cup of mucus a day. Yuck!

Snot and boogers, along with your nose hairs, are like glue traps. They clean the air you breathe by trapping dirt and germs. Dirt and germs get stuck in the mucus before they get into your lungs.

Mucus is normally clear in color. It turns brown, yellow, or green because of the junk it traps and keeps from getting into your lungs.

Your mucus also turns green if you have a sinus infection.

DISCUSSION QUESTIONS

1. If Eek and Ack conquered Earth, which brother would you rather have bossing you around? Why? How are Eek and Ack different?

2. Eek and Ack want to make Earthlings do their chores. Do you have chores that you wish someone else would do? Why? Who would you make do them?

3. Eek and Ack's plan to conquer Earth doesn't work the way they wanted it to. Did that bother them? Do plans always have to turn out the way you want them to? Why or why not?

WRITING PROMPTS

1. Imagine that you are Eek and Ack's older sibling, Ick. Describe how you would help your younger brothers conquer Earth.

2. Eek and Ack try again and again to conquer Earth. Do you have a goal that you try hard to achieve? What is it? Describe your goal and how you try to accomplish it.

3. In this story, the asteroid belt between Mars and Jupiter was created when Eek and Ack destroyed the make-believe planet Zumba. Sometimes writers make up stories to explain things in our world, such as storms, earthquakes, and rainbows. Write your own imaginary story to explain why something happens in the real world.

INTERNET SITES

Do you want to know more about subjects related to this book? Or are you interested in learning about other topics? Then check out FactHound, a fun, easy way to find Internet sites.

Our investigative staff has already sniffed out great sites for you!

Here's how to use FactHound:

1. Visit www.facthound.com

2. Select your grade level.

3. To learn more about subjects related to this book, type in the book's ISBN number: **1598893157**.

4. Click the **Fetch It** button.

FactHound will fetch the best Internet sites for you!

JAN   2008